Granny's Ghost and the Poisoned Punch

Ghostly Gumshoe Cozy Mysteries Series, Volume 2

Sloane Finley

Published by Ginger and Spice Publishing, 2025.

This is a work of fiction. Similarities to real people, places, or events are entirely coincidental.

GRANNY'S GHOST AND THE POISONED PUNCH

First edition. July 11, 2025.

ISBN: 979-8231581771

Written by Sloane Finley.

Table of Contents

Chapter 1

I stand in the middle of my grandmother's—no, *my*—living room, surveying the organized chaos around me. Streamers drape elegantly from the ornate crown molding, their pastel hues a stark contrast to the deep, rich tones of the antique furniture. The scent of lemon furniture polish mingles with the aroma of freshly baked cookies wafting from the kitchen. It's almost perfect, but something still feels off.

"The doilies, dear," a familiar voice chimes in, causing me to jump slightly. "You've forgotten Aunt Gertie's crocheted doilies."

I turn to face the shimmering form of my grandmother, Ingrid, hovering near the fireplace. Even as a ghost, she manages to look both regal and cozy in her favorite floral housecoat. "Granny, I told you, doilies aren't really in style anymore."

She tuts, floating closer to inspect the refreshment table. "Nonsense. A proper party always has doilies. Why, I remember the housewarming your grandfather and I threw back in '62. Every flat surface had a doily, and people raved about it for weeks!"

I can't help but smile, imagining a younger version of my grandmother fussing over doily placement. "I'm sure they did, Granny. But times have changed. I want this party to feel... fresh. Modern."

"Modern," she scoffs, but there's a twinkle in her translucent eyes. "In my day, we knew how to throw a proper shindig. Remember, the secret is in the punch. My special recipe—"

"Is in the family cookbook. I know," I interrupt, my smile growing even wider. "Don't worry, I'll be using it. Some traditions are worth keeping."

Granny beams at me, and for a moment, I swear I can almost feel the warmth of her pride. Then her expression shifts to one of concern. "Now, about your guest list. Are you sure inviting that Dahl fellow is wise? After all the trouble he caused..."

I sigh, setting down the recipe card and smoothing out a non-existent wrinkle in the tablecloth. "Victor Dahl is... complicated. But he's also an important part of the community. If I'm going to make this work—make this house my home—I need to at least try to mend fences."

My mind wanders back to the events of the past few months. Victor Dahl, with his slick suits and slicker words, had been a thorn in my side from the moment I inherited Granny's house. His development company had grand plans for the historic district of New Oslo, plans that would have seen this beautiful old Victorian torn down and replaced with "modern living spaces."

This party, this olive branch, is my attempt to move past that conflict.

"I just hope he doesn't try anything underhanded," Granny mutters, interrupting my reverie.

I shake my head, trying to dispel the lingering doubts. "That's why I'm inviting him, Granny. In the open, where everyone can see. No secrets, no schemes. Just neighbors trying to get along."

Granny doesn't look convinced, but she nods slowly. "Well, you always were a peacemaker, even as a child. I suppose if anyone can smooth things over with that man, it's you."

Her words bolster my confidence, and I stand a little straighter. "Exactly. This party is about new beginnings. For me, for this house, and hopefully, for my relationship with the whole town—Victor Dahl included."

As I put the finishing touches on the refreshment table, carefully arranging a vase of fresh-cut flowers from Granny's garden, I can't shake the feeling that tonight will be a turning point. For better or worse, this housewarming party will set the tone for my new life in New Oslo.

The doorbell chimes, its melodic tones echoing through the house. I glance at the ornate grandfather clock in the corner—still an hour before the party is set to begin. Granny's spectral form flickers with curiosity as I make my way to the front door.

I open it to find Margo Winters on the doorstep, a bright smile plastered on her face. She's clutching a casserole dish like it's a shield.

"Lena, darling!" she trills, stepping inside without waiting for an invitation. "I thought I'd pop by early to lend a hand. You must be absolutely swamped, preparing for such a big event all by yourself."

I force a smile, trying to match her enthusiasm. "That's very kind of you, Margo, but I've got everything under control."

She's already bustling past me, her floral perfume leaving a cloying trail in her wake. "Nonsense! There's always something to be done. Now, where shall I put this lovely spinach and artichoke dip I've brought?"

As I guide her to the kitchen, I catch sight of Granny's ghost rolling her eyes dramatically. I have to stifle a laugh—it seems some neighborly dynamics transcend even death.

Margo sets her dish down and immediately begins rearranging the appetizer platters I'd so carefully laid out. "You know," she says, not looking up from her self-appointed task, "I've always loved this house. Such charm, such history. It's a blessing that you came back to town after your dear grandmother passed. There was talk of it going to auction if none of Ingrid's heirs came back to claim it—can you imagine?"

There's an edge to her voice that makes me pause. I remember the numerous times Margo had tried to convince Granny to sell the place over the years. "Well, I'm here now," I say, perhaps a bit more firmly than necessary. "And I'm looking forward to making this house my home."

Margo's smile tightens almost imperceptibly. "Of course, dear. We're all so... thrilled to have you back in New Oslo."

As Margo continues to "help" by completely redesigning my carefully planned layout, I excuse myself to check on the punch. In the kitchen, I find Granny's ghost hovering over the old family cookbook, open to a well-worn page.

"Your great-great-grandmother's famous punch recipe," she says, her translucent finger pointing to the yellowed paper. "It's been the talk of every party for generations. You simply must use it tonight."

I lean in, squinting at the faded handwriting. The list of ingredients is familiar enough—fruit juices, ginger ale, a hint of cinnamon—but there's something else scrawled in the margin. "Granny, what's this note about a 'secret ingredient'?"

Granny's ghostly form shivers with delight. "Ah, that's what made it special! A tiny pinch of an herb blend, passed down through the women in our family. Said to bring good fortune and smooth over any conflicts among the drinkers. Heaven knows you could use a bit of that tonight."

I raise an eyebrow, intrigued despite my skepticism. "And where would I find this magical herb blend?"

She gestures to a small, ornate box on top of the refrigerator. "In there, dear. Been in the family for generations. Just a pinch, mind you. Too much and, well..." She trails off, a mischievous glint in her eye.

Against my better judgment, I find myself reaching for the box. The idea of a little extra "luck" tonight is too tempting to pass up. As I carefully mix the punch according to the recipe, adding just a pinch of the mysterious herb blend, I can't help but feel a spark of excitement. Maybe there's something to these old family traditions after all.

With the punch prepared and chilling in the refrigerator, I return to the living room to find Margo still fussing over the decorations. Granny's ghost hovers nearby, her expression uncharacteristically somber.

"Lena, dear," she says, her voice low even though I know Margo can't hear her. "I've been thinking about your guest list. Are you certain about some of the people you've invited? There are... tensions, histories you might not be aware of."

I frown, keeping my voice down as I pretend to adjust a flower arrangement. "What do you mean, Granny? Is this about Victor again?"

She shakes her head, her form flickering with agitation. "Not just him. There are others... old grudges, buried secrets. This house has seen its share of drama over the years, and some wounds never truly heal."

"Granny, you're being cryptic," I whisper, growing frustrated. "If you know something, just tell me."

But she merely sighs, a sound like a soft breeze. "It's not my place to dig up old bones, dear. Just... be careful tonight. Keep your eyes open. Not everyone here tonight will be as they seem."

Before I can press her further, Margo calls out from across the room. "Lena, darling, where ever did you find these charming little canapé plates? They look positively antique!"

I turn to answer Margo, but when I glance back, Granny's ghost has vanished. Her warning lingers in the air, mixing uneasily with the scent of lemon polish and fresh flowers. As the clock ticks closer to the party's start time, I can't shake the feeling that tonight will bring more than just a simple housewarming.

Chapter 2

The doorbell chimes, and I feel a flutter of butterflies in my stomach. This is it. My housewarming party is about to begin. I smooth down my dress, take a deep breath, and open the door with what I hope is a welcoming smile.

"Lena, darling! Let me be the first to congratulate you properly!" Margo Winters sweeps in, air-kissing both my cheeks before I can even greet her. She's carrying a suspiciously heavy-looking tote bag. "Now, where shall I set up?"

I blink, momentarily thrown off balance. "Set up?"

"The punch, of course!" Margo laughs, already making her way towards the kitchen. "I brought my antique crystal punch bowl. It'll add just the right touch of elegance to your lovely... rustic decor."

Before I can protest, more guests arrive, and I'm caught up in a whirlwind of greetings and small talk. Mrs. Peterson from the library hands me a beautifully wrapped book. My old English teacher, Mrs. Abernathy, compliments the fresh paint in the entryway.

Then, I see him. Victor Dahl, looking somewhat out of place in his crisp suit among the more casually dressed townspeople. Our eyes meet, and for a moment, the chatter around us seems to fade away. I'd invited him in hopes of burying the hatchet, but now that he's here, I'm not sure if it was the right decision.

"Lena," he says, nodding politely as he approaches. "Thank you for the invitation. Your home looks... charming."

I force a smile. "Thank you, Victor. I'm glad you could make it."

There's an awkward pause, the weight of our past conflicts hanging in the air between us. I'm saved from having to make small talk by the arrival of Dr. Marcus Holloway, the town's physician.

"Good evening, Lena," he says warmly, handing me a bottle of wine. "I hope this pairs well with whatever delightful spread you've prepared."

As more guests filter in, the house begins to buzz with conversation and laughter. I find myself constantly moving, greeting newcomers, accepting housewarming gifts, and trying to keep an eye on everything at once. It's overwhelming, but there's an undercurrent of excitement. This is my new beginning, my chance to establish myself in New Oslo beyond just being "Ingrid's granddaughter."

I catch a glimpse of Granny's ghost hovering near the punch bowl, her transparent form invisible to the other guests. She gives me an encouraging nod, and I feel a surge of confidence. I can do this.

As the party gains momentum, I find myself circulating through the rooms, making sure everyone has drinks and trying to engage in conversation with as many guests as possible. It's exhausting but exhilarating at the same time.

"Lena, this old place scrubs up well, doesn't it?" Mrs. Abernathy comments, running her hand along the polished banister. "Your grandmother would be proud."

I smile, touched by her words. "Thank you, Mrs. Abernathy. I hope I can do it justice."

As I turn to respond to another guest's question about the original stained glass windows, I notice Margo has taken complete control of the drink station. She's ladling punch into glasses with flourish, chatting animatedly with everyone who approaches.

"You simply must try this punch," I overhear her saying to Mrs. Peterson. "It's absolutely divine."

The punch. I have my own cup somewhere, but I can't remember where I might have set it down. Before I can go look for it, I'm waylaid by Victor, who's been hovering on the periphery of the party.

"Lena," he says, his voice low. "I was hoping we could have a word in private."

I hesitate, glancing around at the bustling party. "Victor, I'm not sure this is the best time-"

"It won't take long," he insists, already steering me towards a quiet corner. "I wanted to discuss a new development proposal that I think you'll find very interesting."

My heart sinks. So much for burying the hatchet. "Victor, I thought I made it clear. The house isn't for sale."

He holds up his hands placatingly. "Hear me out. This could be beneficial for both of us. The town, even."

Before I can respond, there's a commotion from the main room. I excuse myself quickly, relieved for the interruption but worried about what's causing the disturbance.

As I push through the crowd, I see Dr. Holloway kneeling beside someone on the floor. My breath catches in my throat when I realize it's Evelyn Blackwood, the town's self-proclaimed psychic. Her eyes are closed, and she's mumbling incoherently.

"Give her some space," Dr. Holloway commands, and the partygoers step back, forming a circle around them.

I kneel down beside them. "What happened?"

Dr. Holloway shakes his head, looking puzzled. "She just collapsed. Evelyn? Can you hear me?"

Evelyn's eyes flutter open, unfocused and glassy. "The house," she mutters. "The house knows. It remembers."

A chill runs down my spine. What on earth is she talking about?

As Dr. Holloway helps Evelyn to her feet, I notice the party has taken on a subdued tone. Guests are whispering among themselves, throwing curious glances our way. I need to get things back on track.

"Everyone," I call out, trying to keep my voice steady. "Evelyn's fine, just a little overwhelmed by the, um, energy of the house." I force a laugh, hoping to lighten the mood. "How about we all try some of that famous punch Margo's been serving up?"

There's a murmur of agreement, and slowly, the party begins to regain its earlier jovial atmosphere. I escort Evelyn to a comfortable chair, making sure she has a glass of water and is feeling better before I return to my hosting duties.

As I make my rounds, I overhear snippets of conversation that make me uneasy.

"...heard it might go to auction," one guest whispers.

"...wonder how she affords the upkeep," another muses.

I spot Dr. Holloway deep in conversation with Victor, their heads bent close together. When they notice me approaching, they quickly separate, Victor smoothing down his tie while Dr. Holloway gives me a tight smile.

"Lena," Dr. Holloway says, his tone casual but his eyes sharp. "Quite the gathering you've put together. I couldn't help but overhear some talk about the house potentially going to auction. Surely that's just idle gossip?"

I feel my chest tighten at his words. "Auction? No, that's not... where did you hear that?"

He shrugs, taking a sip of his punch. "Oh, you know how people talk in small towns. I'm sure it's nothing to worry about."

I force a laugh, trying to sound more confident than I feel. "You're right, it's nothing but gossip. The house is mine, fair and square. It would only have gone to auction if none of Granny's heirs had turned up. But here I am!" I spread my arms wide, encompassing the room. "Very much present and accounted for."

Dr. Holloway nods, but there's something in his expression that makes me wonder if he believes me. As he moves away to join another group, I spot Victor watching our interaction from across the room. His gaze is intense, calculating, and I have to suppress a shiver.

I'm about to go and confront him when the doorbell rings again. Grateful for the distraction, I hurry to answer it. Standing on the porch, wrapped in a flowing, colorful shawl, is Evelyn Blackwood. Wait, Evelyn? But she was just...

I whirl around, scanning the room, and sure enough, there's Evelyn, still seated in the chair where I left her. I turn back to the woman on the porch, my mind reeling.

"You must be Lena," the newcomer says, her voice eerily similar to Evelyn's. "I'm Eva, Evelyn's twin sister. I felt a strong psychic pull to be here tonight. May I come in?"

Speechless, I step aside to let her enter. As Eva sweeps past me, her eyes seem to look right through me, much like her sister's did earlier.

"My dear," she says, her voice low and dramatic, "the energy in this house is simply pulsating tonight. Can you feel it?"

Before I can respond, she's made her way to Evelyn, the two of them immediately engaged in what looks like an intense psychic conversation. The other guests are staring openly now, and I can practically feel the gossip mill starting to churn.

I close the door, wondering what new complications this unexpected arrival might bring to an already complex evening. As I turn back to the party, I catch sight of Granny's ghost again. She's frowning, her spectral form flickering with what I've come to recognize as agitation.

Something's not right, and I have a feeling this party is about to take a turn I never expected.

Chapter 3

The party is in full swing now, the earlier drama of Evelyn's collapse seemingly forgotten. Laughter and chatter fill the air, and I'm starting to think that maybe, just maybe, this housewarming party might turn out alright after all. That's when Evelyn and her sister Eva corner me near the fireplace, their eyes gleaming with an unsettling intensity that makes me want to take a step back. But I stand my ground. After all, this is my house.

"Lena, darling," Evelyn purrs, her bangle-laden arms gesticulating wildly. "We simply must discuss the extraordinary energy emanating from this property. Have you noticed anything... unusual since you moved in?"

I blink, thrown off by the abrupt change of subject. "Unusual? Like what?"

Eva leans in, her voice dropping to a conspiratorial whisper. "Unexplained noises, perhaps? Objects moving on their own? Or maybe dreams of events you couldn't possibly know about?"

A chill runs down my spine as I think of Granny's ghost and the way I was almost killed by my cousin a few weeks back, but there was nothing magical or mystical about that.

Just greed, mostly.

Still, I keep my face neutral. "Can't say that I have. It's just an old house with some creaky floorboards."

The sisters exchange a meaningful look that sets my teeth on edge. "Oh, it's so much more than that," Evelyn insists. "This house sits at the intersection of powerful ley lines. The psychic energy here is positively potent."

"Ley lines?" I repeat, my confusion evident.

"Earth's natural energy pathways," Eva explains, her hands tracing invisible lines in the air. "They crisscross the globe, and where they intersect, like here, the veil between worlds grows thin."

I resist the urge to glance at Granny's ghost, who I can see hovering just behind the sisters, rolling her eyes dramatically.

"That's... interesting," I manage, trying to sound polite but disinterested. "But I'm not sure what that has to do with my house."

"Everything!" they exclaim in unison, causing me to jump slightly.

Evelyn grabs my hand, her grip surprisingly strong. "Lena, you must allow us to conduct a proper investigation. The secrets this house holds could be of immense value to the paranormal community."

I gently but firmly extract my hand from her grasp. "I appreciate your interest, but I'm not comfortable with any investigations. This is my home, not a research site."

Their faces fall in perfect synchronization, and I can't shake the feeling that their interest goes beyond mere scientific curiosity. Before they can protest further, I excuse myself, claiming hostess duties.

As I move away, I hear Eva mutter to Evelyn, "She doesn't understand the power she's sitting on. We need to find another way."

Their words send a shiver down my spine, and I make a mental note to be wary of the Blackwood sisters in the future.

I'm heading towards the kitchen to check on our dwindling snack supply when Dr. Holloway intercepts me. There's a glint in his eye that puts me on edge.

"Lena," he says, his tone casual but his gaze sharp. "I couldn't help but overhear your conversation with the Blackwood sisters. Fascinating stuff, isn't it? All this talk about the unique properties of your house."

I force a smile. "Yes, they do seem to find it quite fascinating. I'm afraid they might have gotten a little carried away with their theories, though."

Dr. Holloway nods, but I can tell he's not letting this go. "Indeed. Still, it does make one wonder about the potential of this old place. Have you given any thought to your long-term plans for the house?"

My guard immediately goes up. First Victor with his development proposals, now this. "Long-term plans?" I repeat, buying time to formulate a response.

"Yes," he continues smoothly. "A house like this, with its history and unique qualities, could be quite valuable to the right buyer. Or perhaps you've considered turning it into a bed and breakfast? I hear those can be quite profitable, especially in picturesque little towns like this one."

For a split-second, I wonder what granny might think of her house being used as a bed and breakfast. Maybe it's on her behalf that I feel a flash of anger at his presumption. "Dr. Holloway, I appreciate your interest, but my long-term plan is to live here. This is my home, not a business opportunity."

He holds up his hands in a placating gesture. "Of course, of course. I didn't mean to overstep. It's just that a young woman like yourself, taking on the responsibility of such a large, old property... Well, it's a lot to manage on your own."

His words sting, mostly because they touch on my own secret doubts. But I refuse to let him see that. "I assure you, I'm more than capable of managing my inheritance. Now, if you'll excuse me, I need to see to my other guests."

As I turn away, I catch sight of Victor watching our interaction from across the room. There's a calculating look in his eye that makes me wonder if he and Dr. Holloway have been comparing notes.

I'm so lost in thought that I simply keep staring at the two men as they continue their conversation. Time seems to slow down as I watch Victor raise a glass of punch to his lips. He takes a long, deep drink, and then his eyes widen. The glass slips from his fingers, shattering on the hardwood floor. Victor clutches at his throat, his face contorting in pain.

"Victor?" I call out, rushing towards him. "Are you okay?"

He tries to speak, but only a choked gasp comes out. Then, like a tree falling in slow motion, he collapses to the floor.

The room erupts into chaos. Mrs. Peterson screams. Dr. Holloway rushes to Victor's side, shouting for someone to call an ambulance. Margo Winters stands frozen, her face pale as she stares at the spilled punch at Victor's feet.

I kneel beside Victor, my heart pounding. His eyes are wide with fear and pain, his breathing shallow and ragged. Dr. Holloway is checking his pulse, his expression grim.

"What's happening?" I ask, my voice shaking. "Is it... is it the punch?"

Dr. Holloway nods grimly. "I suspect so. We need to get everyone who drank it to a hospital immediately."

As if on cue, Mrs. Abernathy lets out a groan from across the room. She's leaning heavily against the wall, her face ashen. "I don't feel so good," she mumbles before sliding to the floor.

More cries of distress fill the air as other guests begin to feel the effects. It's like watching dominoes fall—one by one, people who partook in the punch are succumbing to whatever poison it contained.

I feel like I'm in a nightmare. This can't be happening. How did my simple housewarming party turn into this disaster?

"Lena!" Dr. Holloway's sharp voice cuts through my panic. "I need you to help me. We need to identify everyone who drank the punch and keep them calm until help arrives."

His words spur me into action. I move through the room, trying to identify who needs help while simultaneously attempting to calm those who are still unaffected but panicking.

"Everything is going to be okay," I say, over and over, not sure if I'm trying to convince my guests or myself. "Help is on the way."

In the distance, I hear sirens approaching. Relief washes over me—professional help is almost here.

The next few minutes are a blur of flashing lights, uniformed paramedics, and a cacophony of urgent voices. My living room has been transformed into a makeshift triage center, with the affected guests being assessed and stabilized.

I stand to the side, feeling helpless as I watch the emergency responders work. Victor is being loaded onto a stretcher, an oxygen mask covering his face. Mrs. Abernathy is sitting up now, looking shaken but alert as a paramedic checks her vitals.

A stern-looking Sheriff Mark approaches me, his notebook already out. "Lena? It seems like trouble just follows you around.

I need to ask you a few questions about what happened here tonight."

I nod numbly, still in shock. "Of course. Whatever you need."

As Sheriff Mark begins his questioning, I notice a commotion near the punch bowl. A team in hazmat suits has arrived and is carefully collecting samples of the remaining punch and examining the glasses.

"Sheriff," one of them calls out, holding up a glass vial. "We've got confirmation. There are traces of a toxic substance in these glasses. We'll need to run more tests to identify it specifically, but it's definitely not something that should be in a party punch."

The sheriff's eyebrows shoot up, and he turns back to me with a more intense expression. "Lena, did you prepare this punch yourself?"

"I... no," I stammer. "I mean, I found the recipe in my grandmother's old cookbook, but Margo—Mrs. Winters—she insisted on taking charge of serving it."

Officer Daniels makes a note in his book. "And where is Mrs. Winters now?"

I look around, realizing for the first time that Margo is nowhere to be seen. "I... I don't know. She was here just a few minutes ago."

The officer's expression hardens. "We'll need to speak with her. In the meantime, I'm afraid we'll have to ask everyone who isn't sick to remain here for questioning."

As he walks away to talk with the hazmat people, I become acutely aware of the atmosphere in the room. The initial panic has subsided, replaced by a tense, wary silence. And then I notice the looks.

Suspicious glances are being cast in my direction from all corners of the room. Mrs. Peterson is whispering behind her hand to another guest, both of them eyeing me nervously. Even Dr. Holloway, as he speaks with a paramedic, keeps shooting questioning looks my way.

The weight of their stares makes me feel like I'm suffocating. They can't possibly think... But of course they can. It's my house, my party, my family's punch recipe.

I catch sight of Granny's ghost hovering near the fireplace. Her expression is one of concern and frustration—I can tell she wants to help, to explain, but she's powerless to communicate with anyone but me.

As the last of the affected guests are taken to waiting ambulances, I'm left standing in my living room, surrounded by police, suspicious neighbors, and the tattered remains of what was supposed to be a new beginning.

Chapter 4

The insistent pounding on my front door jolts me awake. For a blissful moment, I can't remember why I feel so awful. Then the events of last night come crashing back, and my stomach lurches. I stumble out of bed, throw on a robe, and make my way downstairs.

Sheriff Mark is standing on my porch, his expression grim. "Morning, Lena. We need to talk."

I step aside to let him in, my mind racing. "Of course, Sheriff. How... how is everyone?"

Mark's face tightens. "Most of the affected guests are stable, but Victor Dahl... he's in critical condition. The doctors aren't sure he'll make it."

The news hits me like a physical blow. I sink onto the sofa, my legs suddenly unable to support me. "Oh my goodness," I whisper.

Mark sits across from me, his notebook already out. "Lena, I'm going to be straight with you. You're our prime suspect right now."

I stare at him, momentarily speechless. "What? But... why?"

He sighs, looking uncomfortable. "Your history with Victor is well-known in town. The property disputes, the back and forth over your grandmother's will... And it was your party, your punch recipe."

"But I didn't even serve the punch!" I protest. "Margo Winters took over—"

Mark holds up a hand to stop me. "I know. We're looking into Mrs. Winters as well. But the fact remains, you had the most obvious motive."

I feel like I'm drowning. "Sheriff, I swear to you, I had nothing to do with this. Yes, Victor and I have had our differences, but I would never... I could never..."

"I want to believe you, Lena," Mark says softly. "But right now, the evidence isn't in your favor. The labs confirmed that the poison was specifically concentrated in Victor's glass. He seems to have been the main target."

My mind whirls. If Victor was the target, doesn't that clear me? Surely I wouldn't have poisoned the entire punch bowl if I was only after Victor. But even as I open my mouth to argue this point, I realize how it sounds. Like I've thought through the logistics of poisoning someone.

Mark continues, his voice taking on an official tone. "I'm going to need you to stay in town and make yourself available for further questioning. We'll also need to search the house."

I nod numbly, too overwhelmed to argue. As Mark begins his search, I sit on the sofa, feeling more alone than I ever have in my life.

The moment Sheriff Mark leaves, Granny's ghost materializes beside me. Her usually cheerful face is creased with worry. "Lena, my dear, we need to talk."

I look up at her, feeling utterly lost. "Granny, what am I going to do? They think I did this!"

She sits—or rather, floats—next to me on the sofa. "Now, you listen to me, sweetie. You are not going to sit here feeling sorry for yourself. You're going to clear your name."

Her firm tone, so familiar from my childhood, snaps me out of my stupor. "But how? The sheriff thinks I had motive, and it was my party, our family's punch recipe—"

"Details!" Granny waves a spectral hand dismissively. "What we need are facts. And to get those, we need to do some investigating of our own."

I stare at her, incredulous. "You want me to play detective? Again?"

"Who better?" Granny argues. "You did a fantastic job before. And you know these people, Lena. You can talk to them in a way the police can't. And you have an advantage they don't." She points to herself with a wink.

Despite everything, I feel a small smile tugging at my lips. "A ghost sidekick?"

"Precisely!" Granny beams. "Now, let's think this through. Who had access to that punch bowl? Who was acting suspiciously? We need to make a list of suspects."

As we brainstorm, I begin to feel a glimmer of hope. Maybe, just maybe, we can figure this out.

"Alright," I say, looking down at the list we've compiled. "So our main suspects are Dr. Holloway, the Blackwood sisters, and Margo Winters."

Granny nods approvingly. "Good start. Now, you'll need to question each of them carefully. Remember, you're not accusing anyone—you're just a concerned hostess checking on your guests after a terrible accident."

I raise an eyebrow at her. "You seem to know a lot about this, Granny. Should I be worried about your past?"

She chuckles. "Let's just say I didn't spend all my time baking cookies, dear. Now, let's think about approach. Dr. Holloway first, I think. You can claim a check-up after the stress of last night."

I nod, jotting down notes. "And the Blackwood sisters?"

"Trickier," Granny muses. "But they seemed very interested in the house. Perhaps you could invite them over to discuss their theories about ley lines?"

"Clever," I admit. "And Margo?"

"Oh, I'm sure she'll come to you," Granny says with a knowing look. "That woman never could resist a bit of drama. When she does, be sympathetic but observant."

As we finalize our plan, I feel a mix of determination and apprehension. I got lucky the last time I had to do some detective work with Granny, but this is different. What if I mess it up? What if I make myself look even more suspicious?

Granny, seeming to sense my doubts, places a cool, ethereal hand on my shoulder. "You can do this, Lena. You're smarter than you give yourself credit for. And remember, I'll be with you every step of the way. Well, in spirit, mostly."

I groan at the pun, but her confidence bolsters mine. "Okay," I nod, taking a deep breath. "Let's do this."

As we prepare for our investigation, Granny's eyes take on a distant look—one I've come to associate with her delving into memories.

"You know," she begins, her voice taking on a gossipy tone I remember well from my childhood, "these folks have always had their secrets. Take Dr. Holloway, for instance. Did you notice how he kept glancing at his watch during the party? And not in a 'I'm bored' way, but like he was waiting for something."

I frown, thinking back. "Now that you mention it, he did seem a bit distracted."

Granny nods. "And it's not the first time I've seen him act oddly. Years ago, there was a town meeting about expanding the medical center. Marcus was dead set against it, which seemed strange for a doctor, don't you think?"

She continues, warming to her subject. "Then there's Evelyn and Eva Blackwood. Those two have always been... overly interested in this house. During the party, I saw Eva sneaking around upstairs. She muttered to herself something about looking for the bathroom, but I don't buy it."

"What?" I exclaim. "Why didn't you tell me this last night?"

Granny has the grace to look sheepish. "Well, dear, there was rather a lot going on, wasn't there? But it's not just that. I overheard them whispering about some kind of 'convergence' happening soon. Sounded ominous, if you ask me."

I make a mental note to ask the sisters about this 'convergence' when I speak to them.

"And Margo," Granny continues, her tone turning disapproving. "That woman was hovering around the punch bowl all night like a bee around a flower. But here's the thing—I saw her slip into the kitchen several times when you weren't looking. And each time, she came out looking... satisfied. Like she'd accomplished something."

My mind races with this new information. Could Margo have been tampering with the punch? But why?

"Granny," I say slowly, "is there anything else you saw? Anything at all that might be important?"

She pauses, thinking. "Well, now that you mention it... I did notice something odd about the punch bowl itself."

I lean forward, eager to hear more. "What about the punch bowl, Granny?"

She furrows her brow, concentrating. "Well, you see, being a ghost has its advantages. I can observe without being noticed. And I saw several guests approach the punch bowl when no one else was around."

"Who?" I ask, grabbing a pen to take notes.

"Let's see... There was Dr. Holloway, of course. He ladled himself a glass, but then he paused, looked around, and made a move toward the bowl, but then someone walked in front of him and blocked my view. I saw him slip something into his pocket when the other guest moved out of the way, though."

My eyes widen. "Are you sure?"

Granny nods firmly. "As sure as I am that I'm dead, dear. Then there was Eva Blackwood. She didn't take any punch, but she was examining the bowl very closely when she thought no one was looking. Even ran her fingers along the rim, muttering something under her breath."

I jot this down, my mind whirling with possibilities. "Anyone else?"

"Yes, Margo, of course. But we knew she had access, since she was serving. However, at one point, I saw her switch out the ladle for a different one. Seemed odd at the time, but I didn't think much of it until... well, until everything happened."

I sit back, overwhelmed by this new information. "So, basically, several of our suspects had unsupervised access to the punch and glasses. Any one of them could have added something to the mix."

Granny nods gravely. "Exactly, dear. Which is why you need to tread carefully. Remember, you're not accusing anyone. You're just gathering information."

I take a deep breath, feeling the weight of the task ahead. "Right. No pressure or anything."

Granny gives me an encouraging smile. "You can do this, Lena. You're my granddaughter, after all. We don't back down from a challenge."

As I stand up, ready to begin my investigation, I can't help but feel a mix of determination and fear. I'm about to start poking around in my neighbors' secrets, and I have a feeling some of them won't appreciate it. But what choice do I have? If I don't clear my name, I could lose everything—my freedom, my home, my future in New Oslo.

Chapter 5

I'm barely through my first cup of coffee the next morning when the doorbell rings. Taking a deep breath, I open the door to find Margo Winters on my porch, a sympathetic smile plastered on her face.

"Lena, darling," she coos, sweeping past me into the house. "I just had to come check on you after that dreadful business at your party. You poor thing, you must be beside yourself!"

I force a smile, reminding myself of Granny's advice. Be sympathetic but observant. "Thank you, Margo. It's been... challenging."

Margo makes herself comfortable on my sofa, patting the spot next to her. "Sit, dear. Tell me everything."

As I settle beside her, I notice her eyes darting around the room, taking in every detail. It's not the first time I've caught her examining the house so intently.

"Margo," I begin carefully, "you've always seemed so interested in this place. Why is that?"

She laughs, a tinkling sound that doesn't quite reach her eyes. "Oh, you know me. I'm just a sucker for old houses. This one, though... it's special."

"Special how?" I probe.

Margo's gaze turns wistful. "It's the crown jewel of New Oslo, Lena. The history, the architecture... they don't make them like this anymore. I've always thought it deserved to be preserved, shared with the community."

I raise an eyebrow. "Shared? You mean, like a museum?"

"Or a bed and breakfast," Margo says, her eyes lighting up. "Can't you just see it? Tourists from all over, coming to experience a piece of New Oslo history."

As she speaks, I begin to understand. Margo doesn't just admire the house—she covets it. The realization sends a chill down my spine.

"You know," I say casually, "Granny mentioned you'd expressed interest in buying the place before."

Margo's smile falters for a split second before returning full force. "Oh, ages ago. Just a passing fancy, really."

But I can see it in her eyes—there's nothing 'passing' about Margo's desire for my home.

As Margo chatters on about the house's potential, my mind drifts back to a conversation I had with Granny years ago. I was just a teenager, visiting for the summer, when I overheard raised voices from Granny's study.

"For the last time, Margo, the house is not for sale!" Granny's voice, usually so kind, was sharp with frustration.

"Be reasonable, Ingrid," Margo's tone was cajoling. "You're not getting any younger. This place is too much for you to manage on your own. My offer is more than fair."

I crept closer to the partially open door, curiosity overcoming my better judgment.

Granny's laugh was cold. "Fair? You're offering half of what this property is worth, and we both know it. Besides, money isn't the issue. This house has been in my family for generations. I intend to keep it that way."

"But your family doesn't appreciate it like I do," Margo argued. "Your children have moved away, your grandchildren hardly visit. I would cherish this house, Ingrid. I would restore it to its former glory."

"My family's appreciation or lack thereof is none of your concern," Granny snapped. "And I'll thank you to stop snooping around my property. Yes, I've seen you, Margo. Taking measurements, peeking in windows. It stops now."

There was a tense silence, and then Margo spoke, her voice low and intense. "You'll regret this, Ingrid. One day, you'll realize I'm right. This house deserves better than to be a forgotten family heirloom."

I heard footsteps approaching and quickly ducked into a nearby room. Margo stormed past, her face flushed with anger. From that day on, there was always a tension between Granny and Margo, a forced politeness that never quite hid the underlying conflict.

Coming back to the present, I study Margo with new eyes. How far would she go to get her hands on this house?

"Lena? Are you listening, dear?" Margo's voice cuts through my reverie.

I shake off the memory and focus on her. "Sorry, Margo. It's been a stressful few days. You were saying?"

She waves a hand dismissively. "Oh, never mind that. I was just wondering if the police have made any progress. It's all so shocking, isn't it? To think, someone at your lovely party was a... well, a poisoner!"

I watch her carefully as I respond. "They're still investigating. Actually, I wanted to ask you about that night. You were handling the punch, weren't you?"

For a split second, I see a flash of something—anger? Fear? Guilt?—in Margo's eyes. But it's gone so quickly I almost think I imagined it.

"Oh yes, I was happy to help with that," she says smoothly. "But you know, I was so busy serving that I hardly had time to do anything else. I tried to be at that punch bowl all night, greeting guests, making sure everyone had a full glass. But I'm afraid I spent a good amount of time moving around the parlor and dining room, checking in on people." She gives me a pointed look. "I know it was a lot for you to play hostess on your own. I was happy to help."

I nod, trying to look convinced. "Of course. It's just, with everything that happened, the police are questioning everyone who had access to the punch."

Margo leans forward, patting my hand. "Darling, I completely understand. And I'm more than happy to tell the police the same thing. I was serving punch and mingling with your other guests all night, right up until... well, until all the unpleasantness started. Plenty of guests can vouch for my whereabouts."

It's a decent alibi, I guess. I sigh to myself, wishing I was better at this stuff.

"That's very helpful, Margo. Thank you," I say. "Oh, and thank you again for all your help setting up before the party. I don't know how I would have managed without you."

Margo beams. "Oh, it was my pleasure, dear. Happy to help with the decorations and setting out the glasses and... um, what else did I do again?"

I keep my face neutral, but internally, I'm on high alert. Margo hadn't helped with the decorations or the glasses. She'd arrived just as the party was starting, insisting on taking over the punch bowl. Why would she lie about that?

"You know, I can't quite remember everything myself," I say lightly. "It was such a busy day."

Margo nods enthusiastically. "Yes, yes, such a whirlwind. Well, I should be going. Do let me know if you need anything, won't you?"

As I show her out, my mind is racing.

After she leaves, I find myself staring out the window, watching her walk down the street. On an impulse, I decide to follow her. I wait a few minutes, then slip out of the house, trying to look casual as I stroll in the same direction Margo took.

I spot her just as she's turning the corner onto her street. Keeping my distance, I follow, not entirely sure what I'm hoping to find. As I near Margo's house, I see her wheeling her trash can to the curb. She glances around furtively before lifting the lid and shoving something down into the bin.

My curiosity piqued, I wait until Margo goes back inside before approaching her trash can. I know it's wrong, possibly illegal, but I can't shake the feeling that Margo is hiding something. Quickly, I lift the lid and peer inside.

Right on top is a glossy brochure. I fish it out, my heart pounding. It's from a real estate company, specializing in historic properties. The brochure is filled with information about turning old homes into profitable bed and breakfasts.

As I stare at the brochure, my mind whirling, I hear a door open. Panicking, I shove the brochure into my pocket and hurry away, trying to look nonchalant. Once I'm safely around the corner, I lean against a tree, breathing heavily.

What does this mean? Is Margo still actively trying to get her hands on my house? And how far would she go to make that happen?

Back at home, I slump onto the sofa, my head spinning with everything I've learned. Granny's ghost appears beside me, her expression concerned.

"You look troubled, dear. Did your talk with Margo not go well?"

I fill Granny in on my conversation with Margo and my impulsive dumpster dive. As I speak, Granny's frown deepens.

"That Margo," she mutters. "Always poking her nose where it doesn't belong. You know, this reminds me of something that happened years ago, not long after that argument you overheard."

I sit up straighter, intrigued. "What happened?"

Granny's eyes take on that faraway look she gets when she's delving into old memories. "It was late one night. I couldn't sleep, so I came downstairs for some tea. As I passed by the window, I saw a figure in the garden. At first, I thought it was just shadows playing tricks on my eyes, but then I realized it was Margo."

"What was she doing?" I ask.

"She was digging," Granny says, her voice low. "Right by the old oak tree. I watched her for a while, not sure what to make of it. Finally, I opened the window and called out to her. You should have seen her jump! She stammered something about losing an earring earlier that day, but I knew she was lying."

I lean forward, captivated. "Did you ever find out what she was really doing?"

Granny shakes her head. "No, but the next day, I noticed the soil had been disturbed in several places around the property. It was like she was searching for something."

"But what?" I wonder aloud.

"I don't know," Granny admits. "But after that night, Margo's attempts to buy the house became more... aggressive. She started spreading rumors in town that I couldn't manage the upkeep, that the house was falling into disrepair. She even tried to get the historical society involved, claiming I wasn't preserving the property properly. Margo Winters has wanted this house for a very long time. And in my experience, people with that kind of obsession can be dangerous."

As I ponder Granny's words, I can't help but feel a chill. What secrets does this house hold that would drive Margo to such lengths? And more importantly, what might she do next in her quest to possess it?

I glance at the real estate brochure peeking out of my pocket. One thing's for sure—my investigation is far from over. Margo Winters may have provided an alibi, but she's also raised a host of new questions. And I intend to find the answers.

Chapter 6

I stand outside Dr. Holloway's office, my heart pounding. The "Open" sign swings gently in the breeze, almost mocking me with its cheerful invitation. I take a deep breath, reminding myself why I'm here. It's not just about clearing my name anymore; it's about uncovering the truth, no matter where it leads.

Pushing open the door, I'm greeted by the familiar smell of antiseptic and the soft hum of fluorescent lights. The receptionist, Mrs. Baxter, looks up with a smile.

"Lena! What a surprise. Do you have an appointment?"

I force a weak smile. "No, I was hoping Dr. Holloway might have a few minutes. After everything that happened at the party, I've been feeling a bit... off."

Mrs. Baxter's expression softens with sympathy. "Of course, dear. Let me see if he's available."

As she disappears into the back, I take a seat in the waiting room, my eyes darting around for anything unusual. But it's all depressingly normal—outdated magazines, a quietly burbling fish tank, faded posters about the importance of hand-washing.

A few minutes later, Dr. Holloway appears in the doorway. "Lena, come on back. Let's see what's troubling you."

I follow him into the examination room, my mind racing as I try to figure out how to steer the conversation where I need it to go.

Dr. Holloway gestures for me to sit on the examination table. "Now, what seems to be the problem?"

I fidget with the paper covering, buying time. "Well, doctor, I've been having trouble sleeping since the party. I can't stop thinking about what happened, about Victor..."

He nods sympathetically, taking a seat across from me. "That's understandable, Lena. You've been through a traumatic experience. Have you considered talking to a therapist?"

"Actually," I say, seizing the opening, "I find being in the house comforting. It's like... like I can feel Granny's presence there, you know?"

Dr. Holloway's expression flickers with something I can't quite read. Interest? Concern? "The house does seem to have a... unique atmosphere," he says carefully. "I've always found it fascinating."

I lean in slightly. "You have? I remember you asking about my plans for it at the party. Are you interested in old houses, Dr. Holloway?"

He chuckles, but there's a tension in it that wasn't there before. "Oh, you know, just a hobby of mine. Old buildings have such character, such history. Your grandmother's house, in particular, is quite remarkable."

I nod encouragingly, hoping he'll elaborate. "It is. Though sometimes I worry about keeping up with the maintenance. It's a lot for one person to manage."

Dr. Holloway's eyes light up at this. "You know, Lena, if you ever decided you wanted to... explore other options for the property, I'd be happy to discuss some ideas with you."

"Other options?" I repeat, feigning naivety.

He leans forward, his voice taking on an eager tone. "Well, properties like yours can be quite valuable if utilized correctly.

Have you ever considered turning it into a bed and breakfast, for example? Or perhaps a historical tour site?"

I shake my head, watching him carefully. He's the second person in as many days who has suggested turning my grandmother's home—my home—into a bed and breakfast. Am I missing something? Is it really such a no-brainer that I'm the only one who doesn't see it? "I hadn't really thought about it. Do you think there'd be interest in something like that?"

"Oh, absolutely," Dr. Holloway says, his enthusiasm evident. "In fact, I've been doing some research on the subject. It's quite fascinating, really. The potential for properties like yours is enormous."

Our conversation is interrupted by a sharp knock on the door. Mrs. Baxter pokes her head in, looking apologetic.

"I'm sorry to interrupt, Dr. Holloway, but you have an urgent call. They say it can't wait."

Dr. Holloway's face tightens almost imperceptibly. "I see. Lena, would you excuse me for a moment? I'll be right back."

As he leaves the room, I'm torn. Part of me knows I should stay put, be the good patient. But the investigator in me is screaming to seize this opportunity. Before I can second-guess myself, I'm on my feet, creeping towards the partially open door.

Dr. Holloway's voice drifts down the hallway, tense and low. "I told you, I need more time. The investment hasn't paid off yet, but it will. I just need... No, you don't understand. I have a plan. There's this property..."

I strain to hear more, but his voice drops even lower. I catch fragments—"retirement," "one last deal," "everything I have"—before I hear footsteps approaching. I quickly retreat to the examination table, trying to look as innocent as possible.

When Dr. Holloway returns, his smile seems forced. "Sorry about that, Lena. Now, where were we?"

I decide to take a risk. "Actually, Dr. Holloway, I couldn't help overhearing... Is everything okay? You seemed upset."

He waves a hand dismissively, but I notice it's shaking slightly. "Oh, just some business matters. Nothing for you to worry about. Now, about those sleeping problems..."

As he launches into a discussion about relaxation techniques and possible medications, my mind is whirling. What kind of "business matters" could have the town doctor so agitated? And what does it have to do with my house?

As our appointment wraps up, Dr. Holloway seems distracted, his earlier enthusiasm about my house replaced by a preoccupied frown. He scribbles out a prescription for a mild sleeping aid and hands it to me.

"This should help with the insomnia, Lena. And remember, if you ever want to discuss... options for the house, my door is always open."

I thank him and make my way out, but instead of heading straight home, I find myself lingering in the parking lot. Something doesn't add up, and I can't shake the feeling that I'm missing a crucial piece of the puzzle.

As I'm debating my next move, I notice Dr. Holloway emerging from the back of the building, a large trash bag in hand. He deposits it in the dumpster and hurries back inside, glancing around furtively as he goes.

I know it's wrong. I know it's probably illegal. But before I can talk myself out of it, I'm creeping towards the dumpster. Glancing around to make sure no one's watching, I hoist myself up and peer inside.

The bag Dr. Holloway just threw away is right on top. With trembling hands, I open it, my heart pounding in my ears. Inside, I find a stack of papers. Medical bills, loan statements, and... a familiar-looking brochure.

I pull it out, my breath catching in my throat. It's identical to the one I found in Margo's trash—a glossy pamphlet about turning historic homes into profitable businesses. But mixed in with the brochure are documents that paint a troubling picture: past-due notices, threatening letters from creditors, and what looks like a rejected loan application.

As I sift through the papers, a clear narrative begins to emerge. Dr. Holloway is in serious financial trouble. The kind of trouble that might drive a man to desperate measures.

Suddenly, his intense interest in my house takes on a sinister new light. Is he seeing it as a potential lifeline? A way to solve his money problems?

I stuff the brochure and a few of the more damning documents into my purse, my mind racing. Dr. Holloway's financial troubles, his eagerness to discuss "options" for my house, the tense phone call about investments and plans... it all points to a man on the edge, a man who might be willing to do anything to save himself from financial ruin.

Chapter 7

The wind chimes tinkle ominously as I push open the door to "Mystical Pathways," Evelyn Blackwood's new age shop. The air is thick with incense, and I have to blink a few times to adjust to the dim, purple-tinted lighting. I spot Evelyn at the back of the shop, arranging crystals on a velvet-draped table.

"Lena!" she exclaims, gliding towards me with her arms outstretched. "I had a feeling you'd be visiting us today. The spirits are restless, aren't they?"

I force a smile, reminding myself why I'm here. "Hi, Evelyn. I saw you were offering a workshop on... uh, energy cleansing? I thought it might help after everything that's happened."

Evelyn's eyes light up. "Oh, my dear, you've come to the right place. Negative energies can linger after traumatic events. We must cleanse your aura immediately!"

Before I can protest, she's ushering me to a cushion on the floor. Other workshop participants are already seated in a circle, their eyes closed in meditation. I recognize a few faces from town, including Mrs. Peterson from the library and, to my surprise, Deputy Daniels from the local police.

Evelyn takes her place at the head of the circle, raising her arms dramatically. "Welcome, seekers of truth and balance. Today, we will learn to purify our energy fields and connect with the ancient wisdom of the earth."

As Evelyn leads the group through a series of chants and visualizations, I try to stay alert, looking for any clues that might connect her to the poisoning at my party. But it's hard to focus with all the talk of chakras and spirit guides.

Just as I'm starting to wonder if this whole thing is a waste of time, Evelyn fixes her gaze on me. "Lena, dear, I sense a great disturbance in your energy. Would you allow me to perform a personal cleansing ritual?"

All eyes turn to me, and I realize I don't have much choice. "Of course," I say, hoping my nervousness isn't obvious.

Evelyn guides me to stand in the center of the circle. She begins to wave her hands around me, murmuring what sounds like Latin mixed with complete gibberish. Suddenly, she gasps.

"Oh, Lena," she breathes, her eyes wide. "Your house... it's a nexus point. A convergence of powerful ley lines. Do you have any idea what that means?"

I shake my head, genuinely confused.

Evelyn leans in close, her voice dropping to a whisper. "It means your property holds immense power. Power that could be harnessed for great good... or terrible evil. You must be very careful, Lena. There are those who would stop at nothing to control such a nexus."

A chill runs down my spine. Is she warning me? Or threatening me?

As Evelyn continues the "cleansing," she makes more cryptic comments about my house. "The veil is thin there," she murmurs. "The past and present intertwine. Secrets buried long ago are stirring."

By the time the ritual ends, my head is spinning with questions. What does Evelyn know about my house? And how far would she go to access its supposed "power"?

After the workshop, I linger in the shop, pretending to browse while I keep an eye on Evelyn. She's busy with other customers, so I take the opportunity to explore.

The shelves are crammed with an eclectic mix of items: crystals, tarot cards, dream catchers, and books with titles like "Communing with Nature Spirits" and "Ley Lines: The Earth's Hidden Power Grid."

But it's the herb section that really catches my attention. Rows of glass jars line the wall, each filled with dried plants and labeled with both common and Latin names. I recognize some as common cooking herbs—rosemary, thyme, sage—but others are less familiar.

One jar in particular makes me pause. The label reads "Atropa belladonna—Deadly Nightshade." I remember reading about this plant; it's highly toxic, with a long history of use in both medicine and poison.

Next to it, I spot more potentially dangerous plants: "Conium maculatum—Poison Hemlock," "Digitalis purpurea—Foxglove," and "Datura stramonium—Jimsonweed." Each of these, I know, can be lethal if misused.

I'm so engrossed in my discovery that I don't hear Evelyn approach. "Fascinating, aren't they?" her voice makes me jump. "Nature's pharmacy. Healing and harm, all in the same leaf."

I try to keep my voice steady as I respond. "They're certainly interesting. Do you use these in your... rituals?"

Evelyn's smile is enigmatic. "Only the safe ones, of course. But it's important to understand the full spectrum of nature's power. Light and dark, life and death – it's all part of the great balance."

As she speaks, I can't help but wonder: could Evelyn have used one of these plants to poison the punch at my party? The thought sends a shiver down my spine.

"You know," Evelyn continues, her voice taking on a dreamy quality, "your grandmother understood the power of plants. She had quite the herb garden, as I recall."

I perk up at this. "You knew my grandmother well?"

Evelyn's expression turns wistful. "Oh yes, Ingrid and I went way back. She had a gift, you know. A real connection to the earth. It's a shame she never fully embraced her potential."

As Evelyn launches into a story about my grandmother's "untapped psychic abilities," I make a mental note to ask Granny about her history with the Blackwood family. Something tells me there's more to this story than Evelyn is letting on.

The moment I step through my front door, Granny's ghost materializes, her expression anxious. "Well? How did it go with Evelyn?"

I slump onto the sofa, exhausted. "It was... weird. Granny, did you know Evelyn thinks our house is some kind of psychic hotspot?"

Granny rolls her eyes. "Oh, not that nonsense again. I swear, the Blackwood women have been trying to get their hands on this property for generations."

My ears perk up at this. "What do you mean?"

Granny settles into her favorite armchair – or rather, hovers above it in a seated position. "It all started with Evelyn's grandmother, Esmeralda. She was a real piece of work, that one. Claimed to be a psychic medium, always going on about ley lines and energy vortexes."

I lean forward, intrigued. "What did she want with our house?"

"She was convinced there was some sort of 'cosmic portal' in the basement," Granny scoffs. "Kept trying to convince my mother to let her perform rituals here. When Mom refused, Esmeralda started spreading rumors that the house was haunted, cursed even. Said it needed to be 'cleansed' by a true psychic."

"That sounds a lot like what Evelyn was saying today," I muse.

Granny nods grimly. "The apple doesn't fall far from the tree, I suppose. Evelyn's been pulling the same tricks for years. Always hinting at some great power hidden in the house, trying to worm her way in."

A thought occurs to me. "Granny, do you think Evelyn might have had something to do with the poisoning? She has all these dangerous plants in her shop..."

Granny's expression turns thoughtful. "I wouldn't put anything past that woman. But be careful, Lena. The Blackwoods can be dangerous when they don't get what they want."

As I ponder Granny's warning, I can't help but feel that I'm only scratching the surface of a mystery that goes back generations.

The next morning, I decide to do a thorough inspection of the property, looking for any signs of Evelyn's meddling. As I round the corner of the house, something catches my eye.

There, in a flowerbed near the old oak tree, is a small, freshly dug hole. Beside it lies a tiny glass vial, the kind used for collecting scientific samples. My heart racing, I scan the rest of the garden and spot several more disturbed patches of earth, each with a similar vial nearby.

I pick up one of the vials, turning it over in my hand. It's labeled with a date – just two days before my ill-fated housewarming party – and what looks like coordinates.

"What on earth?" I mutter, my mind whirling with possibilities.

I continue my search, finding more evidence of Evelyn's intrusion. Near the back fence, I discover a small, ornate brass object half-buried in the soil. It looks like some sort of compass, but instead of cardinal directions, it's marked with strange symbols.

As I'm examining the compass, a glint of metal catches my eye. Pushing aside some overgrown bushes, I uncover a small digital device, its green light blinking steadily. With a jolt, I realize it's a seismograph – a tool used to measure ground movements.

The pieces start to fall into place. Evelyn hasn't just been spouting new age nonsense; she's been actively investigating the property. But why? What is she hoping to find?

I gather up the vials and equipment, my mind racing. Is this all part of Evelyn's obsession with ley lines and psychic energy? Or is there something more tangible—and potentially valuable. LEAVE NOW, OR FACE THE CONSEQUENCES."

My hands shake as I read the words again and again. It's not just the threat that unnerves me, but the eerily familiar phrasing. "The balance must be restored." Isn't that exactly the kind of thing Evelyn is always going on about?

I burst through the front door, calling for Granny. She appears instantly, her spectral form flickering with concern.

"Lena? What's wrong, dear? You look like you've seen a ghost—and I don't mean me."

I hold out the note with trembling hands. "Someone left this in our mailbox. And look what I found in the garden."

As I show Granny the soil samples and strange devices, her expression grows increasingly grave.

"Oh, Lena," she sighs. "I was afraid something like this might happen. The Blackwoods have never been able to leave well enough alone."

One thing's for certain, this mystery just got a whole lot deeper, and potentially more dangerous.

Chapter 8

The antiseptic smell of the hospital assaults my senses as I step out of the elevator onto Victor's floor. My stomach churns with a mix of anxiety and guilt. The last time I saw Victor, he was being loaded into an ambulance, his face contorted in pain. Now, as I approach his room, I'm not sure what to expect.

I pause outside his door, my hand hovering over the handle. What if he doesn't want to see me? What if he blames me for what happened? Taking a deep breath, I push my doubts aside and knock softly.

"Come in," a weak voice calls from inside.

I enter to find Victor propped up in bed, looking pale and drawn but alert. His eyes widen in surprise when he sees me.

"Lena? I didn't expect to see you here."

I force a smile, trying to hide my nervousness. "Hi, Victor. I... I wanted to see how you were doing. And to apologize."

Victor raises an eyebrow. "Apologize? For what?"

I move closer to the bed, wringing my hands. "For everything. The party, the punch, our past conflicts. I never wanted any of this to happen."

To my surprise, Victor's expression softens. "Lena, you don't need to apologize. Whatever our differences, I know you're not capable of something like this."

His words lift a weight I didn't even realize I was carrying. "Thank you, Victor. That means a lot."

We fall into an awkward silence, years of animosity hanging between us. Finally, I clear my throat. "So, um, how are you feeling?"

Victor grimaces. "Like I've been hit by a truck. But the doctors say I'm improving. Another few days and I should be out of here."

I nod, relieved. "That's good to hear. Is there anything you need? Anything I can do?"

He seems to consider this for a moment. "Actually, there is something I wanted to discuss with you. Something important."

I pull up a chair, curious. "What is it?"

Victor leans forward, his voice dropping to a near whisper. "Lena, I know we've had our differences, especially when it comes to your property. But I need you to know that I'm not your enemy here."

I frown, confused. "What do you mean?"

He sighs, looking troubled. "There's another developer interested in the area. Someone with deep pockets and not a lot of scruples, if you catch my drift."

My mind races. Another developer? "Who is it?" I ask.

Victor shakes his head. "I don't have a name, just rumors. But they've been buying up properties all around your grandmother's house. I think they're trying to pressure you into selling."

I lean back, stunned. "But why? What's so special about my property?"

"I'm not sure," Victor admits. "But whatever it is, it's big. Big enough for someone to resort to dangerous tactics."

As Victor continues to share what he knows about this mysterious rival, I can't help but feel a grudging respect for him. Despite our past conflicts, he's trying to warn me, to help me. It's a side of Victor I've never seen before.

"Thank you for telling me this," I say when he finishes. "I know we haven't always seen eye to eye, but I appreciate your honesty."

Victor nods, looking tired. "Just be careful, Lena. Whoever is behind this, they're playing for keeps."

As I leave the hospital, my mind is whirling with new information and possibilities. The mystery surrounding my house seems to be growing deeper by the minute.

"An outside developer?" Granny's ghost looks skeptical as I recount my conversation with Victor. We're in the living room, where I've just finished filling her in on my hospital visit. "I don't know, Lena. It seems a bit far-fetched."

I pace the room, too agitated to sit still. "But it makes sense, doesn't it? All these people suddenly interested in the house—Dr. Holloway, Margo, the Blackwood sisters. What if they're all working for this mystery developer?"

Granny shakes her head. "That's a pretty big leap, dear. We've known these people for years. The idea that they're all part of some grand conspiracy..."

"Is it really so hard to believe?" I counter. "Think about it. Dr. Holloway is in financial trouble. Margo's always wanted the house. And the Blackwoods are convinced there's some kind of mystical power here. What if someone is playing on their weaknesses, using them to get to us?"

Granny floats over to the window, gazing out at the property. "It's possible, I suppose. But it seems unnecessarily complicated. Why not just make an offer directly?"

I join her at the window, trying to see what she's looking at. "Maybe they did, and Granny Ingrid turned them down. Maybe they're trying to force our hand."

We stand in silence for a moment, both lost in thought. Finally, Granny speaks. "Even if there is an outside culprit, that doesn't explain everything. The poisoning, for instance. That seems very personal, very local."

I have to admit she has a point. "So what do you think is going on?"

Granny turns to me, her spectral form flickering with concern. "I think the truth is probably somewhere in the middle. There might be outside interests at play, but I suspect our local friends are acting on their own motivations as well."

I nod slowly, considering her words. "So we can't rule anyone out."

"Exactly," Granny agrees. "We need to keep our eyes open and consider all possibilities."

As we continue to debate the likelihood of an outside culprit versus local suspects, I can't help but feel we're still missing something crucial. There's a piece of this puzzle we haven't found yet, a connection we're not seeing.

Our discussion is interrupted by a sudden change in Granny's demeanor. She stiffens, her eyes fixed on something outside the window.

"Lena," she says, her voice urgent. "Come look at this."

I hurry to her side, following her gaze. At first, I don't see anything unusual, just the familiar landscape of our property. But then I notice what Granny is pointing at.

There, at the edge of the property line, is a strange symbol carved into the trunk of an old oak tree. It looks like a complex geometric pattern, with swirling lines and sharp angles.

"That wasn't there yesterday," I say, my voice barely above a whisper.

Granny nods grimly. "No, it wasn't. And it's not the only one."

As we scan the property, we spot more markings. They're subtle, easy to miss if you're not looking for them, but once you see one, the others become apparent. Carved into trees, scratched onto rocks, even burned into patches of grass—a network of mysterious symbols surrounding our house.

"What does it mean?" I ask, a chill running down my spine.

Granny shakes her head, looking troubled. "I don't know, Lena. But I have a feeling it's not good. These markings... they remind me of something I've seen before, long ago."

I turn to her, curious. "What? Where?"

But Granny seems lost in thought, her spectral form flickering with agitation. "I can't quite remember. It's like trying to recall a dream. But I know it's important."

As we continue to study the markings, a sense of unease settles over me. These symbols, appearing so suddenly and mysteriously, feel like a message—or a warning. But from whom? And why?

I think back to Victor's words about the rival developer, to the threatening note in our mailbox, to Evelyn's cryptic comments about ley lines and cosmic power. Somehow, I'm sure all of these things are connected. The question is, how?

"We need to document these," I say, reaching for my phone to take pictures. "And then we need to figure out what they mean."

Granny nods in agreement. "Be careful, Lena. Whoever is behind this, they're getting bolder. These markings... they're like a claim on our property. A magical claim."

As I step outside to photograph the symbols, I can't shake the feeling that we've just entered a new phase of this mystery. The stakes are rising, the danger growing. And at the center of it all is our house, holding secrets I'm only beginning to uncover.

Chapter 9

The doorbell rings, and I rush to answer it, relief flooding through me at the sight of Charlie's familiar face. My best friend since forever, Charlie has been my partner in crime-solving before, and I've never been so glad to see her.

"Charlie! Thank God you're here," I say, pulling her into a quick hug.

She grins, holding up a bag full of equipment. "Ready to play detective again, Lena? I borrowed a bunch of stuff from the science lab at the high school."

I can't help but laugh. "They let you just waltz in and take a bunch of equipment?"

Charlie shrugs. "Not a bunch. Just a few things that might come in handy. Being president of the alumni committee comes in handy sometimes, you know."

She cracks me up, and this is exactly why I love having her in my life again.

I lead her to the kitchen, where I've laid out the remaining punch and glasses from the ill-fated party. The police had returned them after their initial investigation, seeing no need to keep them. Their oversight is our gain.

"So, walk me through what happened," Charlie says, pulling on a pair of latex gloves.

As I recount the events of the party, Charlie listens intently, her brow furrowed in concentration. When I finish, she nods slowly.

"Alright, let's start with the punch itself," she says, pulling out a series of test tubes and pipettes.

We work in tandem, Charlie directing me as we take samples from the punch bowl and each of the glasses. The kitchen table becomes a makeshift lab, covered in vials, test strips, and half a dozen other instruments Charlie confiscated from the high school.

We fall into an easy rhythm, our old friendship rekindling as we work. It feels good to have Charlie here, her steady presence a balm to my frayed nerves.

As the tests run, we theorize about potential suspects and motives. Charlie's outsider perspective is invaluable, helping me see connections I might have missed.

Finally, after what feels like hours, Charlie sits back with a triumphant smile. "Lena, I think we've got something."

I lean forward eagerly as Charlie spreads out our test results. "What did you find?"

Charlie points to a series of chemical readouts. "Look here. The punch itself shows no traces of any toxic substances. It's just what it appears to be—a harmless, if rather potent, fruit punch."

My brow furrows in confusion. "But that's impossible. People were definitely poisoned."

"Ah," Charlie says, a glint in her eye, "that's where it gets interesting. Take a look at these results from the glasses."

I scan the papers, my eyes widening as I realize what I'm seeing. "Some of the glasses show traces of toxins, but others don't."

Charlie nods. "Exactly. The poison wasn't in the punch bowl at all. It was added to specific glasses."

The implications of this hit me like a ton of bricks. "So the poisoner wasn't trying to hurt everyone. They had specific targets."

"It seems that way," Charlie agrees. "And it tells us something else, too. Something important about our poisoner."

I think for a moment, then it clicks. "They must have had access to the house before the party. They couldn't have doctored individual glasses during the event without being noticed."

Charlie beams at me. "Bingo. Our culprit isn't just a guest who acted on impulse. This was premeditated. They were in your house, Lena, preparing those glasses in advance."

A chill runs down my spine at the thought of the killer moving through my home, carefully laying their trap. "But who could have had that kind of access?"

We spend the next hour going through the guest list, considering who might have had the opportunity to enter the house before the party. As we debate the merits and motives of each suspect, I can't shake the feeling that we're still missing something. The who and the how are becoming clearer, but the why remains frustratingly elusive.

"Charlie," I say suddenly, a thought occurring to me, "what if this wasn't just about hurting people? What if the poisoning was a distraction?"

Charlie raises an eyebrow. "A distraction from what?"

I shake my head, frustrated. "I don't know. But something about this whole situation feels bigger than just a local dispute. There are too many people interested in this house, too many strange occurrences."

As I fill Charlie in on Victor's warning about the rival developer and the mysterious symbols appearing on the property, her expression grows increasingly serious.

"Lena," she says slowly, "I think you might be onto something. This is starting to sound less like a simple poisoning and more like an actual plot. A conspiracy."

The word hangs in the air between us, heavy with implication. A conspiracy. It sounds ridiculous, like something out of a bad movie. And yet, as I look at the evidence spread out before us, I can't deny that it fits.

"So what do we do now?" I ask, feeling overwhelmed by the scope of what we might be facing.

Charlie squeezes my hand reassuringly. "We keep digging. We follow every lead, no matter how small. And we watch our backs. If this really is a conspiracy, we don't know how far it goes or who might be involved."

As we clean up our makeshift lab, I'm grateful for Charlie's steady presence. Whatever we're up against, at least I'm not facing it alone.

Later that evening, after Charlie has gone home, I'm sitting in the living room, going over our notes for the hundredth time. The house is quiet, save for the ticking of the old grandfather clock in the hall.

Suddenly, my phone buzzes with a text from an unknown number. My heart racing, I open the message:

"If you want answers, watch the old oak at the edge of your property. Midnight meetings. Be careful who you trust."

I stare at the screen, my mind whirling. An anonymous tip? It could be a trap, but it could also be the break we've been looking for.

Before I can decide what to do, Granny's ghost appears, her expression urgent. "Lena, come quickly. There's something you need to see."

I follow her to the back window, peering out into the darkness of the garden. At first, I see nothing. Then, a movement catches my eye.

There, near the old oak tree mentioned in the text, a shadowy figure is moving. They're dressed all in black, their features indistinguishable in the gloom. As I watch, they seem to be examining the trunk of the tree, right where one of the strange symbols had appeared.

"I've been watching for the past hour," Granny whispers, though I know logically that the figure can't hear her. "They've been circling the property, checking all the places where those markings showed up."

My heart pounds as I observe the intruder. Who are they? What are they looking for? And how are they connected to the poisoning, the rival developer, and all the other strange events surrounding my home?

As if sensing they're being watched, the figure suddenly looks up towards the house. I duck down, holding my breath, praying they didn't see me.

When I dare to peek out again, the garden is empty. The shadowy figure has vanished as mysteriously as they appeared.

"What do we do?" I ask Granny, my voice shaking slightly.

Her spectral form flickers with concern. "For now, we wait and watch. But Lena, be careful. I have a feeling things are about to get much more dangerous."

As I head to bed that night, my mind is racing with questions. The anonymous tip, the midnight visitor, the poisoned glasses—how does it all fit together? One thing's for certain: this mystery is far from solved. And as I drift off into an uneasy sleep, I can't shake the feeling that we're on the brink of uncovering something big—something that could change everything.

Chapter 10

The night air is crisp and still as I settle into my makeshift blind, a small tent hidden among the bushes at the edge of the property. It's just past eleven, and I'm armed with a thermos of coffee, night-vision binoculars, and a determination to catch our mysterious intruder.

I've spent the day preparing for this stakeout, carefully planning my vantage point to keep an eye on both the old oak tree and the areas where Granny spotted the shadowy figure. Charlie wanted to join me, but I convinced her to be my backup instead. She's parked down the street, ready to call for help if things go south.

As the minutes tick by, I fight against the encroaching boredom and fatigue. The garden is quiet, almost eerily so. Not even the usual nighttime sounds of crickets or rustling leaves break the silence. It's as if the whole property is holding its breath, waiting.

Just as I'm beginning to wonder if this whole endeavor is a waste of time, movement catches my eye. A figure emerges from the shadows near the property line, their form obscured by a long, dark cloak. My heart races as I raise the binoculars to my eyes.

The figure moves with purpose, gliding across the lawn towards the old oak tree. As they near it, I can make out more details. The cloak is adorned with intricate symbols, similar to the ones we found marked around the property. In one hand, they carry what looks like a gnarled wooden staff.

I watch, transfixed, as the figure reaches the oak tree. They pause, seeming to survey the area, and I shrink back further into my hiding spot. Satisfied they're alone, the cloaked intruder begins to move in a slow, deliberate pattern around the tree.

With growing astonishment, I realize I'm witnessing some sort of ritual. The figure is chanting in a low voice, words I can't make out from this distance. They raise the staff, tracing symbols in the air that glow faintly before fading away.

As the ritual continues, the air seems to thicken, charged with an energy I can almost taste. The hairs on the back of my neck stand up, and I feel a pressure building, like the moment before a thunderstorm breaks.

Just as the tension reaches a crescendo, a twig snaps beneath my foot. The sound, barely audible to my ears, is enough to break the cloaked figure's concentration. They whirl around, scanning the darkness.

I hold my breath, willing myself to become invisible. For a long moment, neither of us moves. Then, with a suddenness that startles me, the figure turns and flees, their cloak billowing behind them as they race towards the woods at the back of the property.

Cursing under my breath, I scramble out of my hiding spot. I can't let them get away, not when I'm so close to answers.

My feet pound against the damp earth as I give chase, my heart thundering in my chest. The cloaked figure is fast, darting between trees with a grace that suggests intimate familiarity with these woods. But I'm no slouch either, years of morning jogs finally paying off as I slowly close the gap between us.

As we plunge deeper into the forest, the branches seem to reach out, snagging at my clothes and hair. I bat them away impatiently, my eyes fixed on the fleeing shape ahead of me. In the darkness, it's hard to make out details, but I catch glimpses of the ornate cloak fluttering in the moonlight that filters through the canopy.

Suddenly, the figure stumbles, caught off guard by a protruding root. They recover quickly, but not before something falls from their grasp, glinting as it hits the forest floor. I make a mental note of the spot, determined to retrieve it once this chase is over.

The pursuit continues, our ragged breathing and the crunch of leaves underfoot the only sounds in the otherwise silent woods. I'm so focused on keeping the figure in sight that I almost don't notice when the trees begin to thin out. We're approaching the edge of the forest, where it gives way to the fields beyond my property.

Just as I think I might finally catch up, the cloaked figure makes a sharp turn. By the time I round the same bend, they've vanished. I skid to a stop, spinning in place as I search desperately for any sign of movement. But the night is still, the fields empty under the pale moonlight.

Frustration and disappointment wash over me. I was so close! Panting, I lean against a tree, trying to catch my breath and gather my thoughts. As my pulse slowly returns to normal, I remember the object the figure dropped. At least the night won't be a total loss.

Retracing my steps proves challenging in the dark woods, but eventually, I find the spot where the intruder stumbled. There, half-buried in the fallen leaves, is a small object. I brush away the debris to reveal a charm, about the size of a silver dollar.

It's made of what looks like tarnished silver, intricately carved with symbols that match those on the cloaked figure's garment.

As I hold the charm up to the moonlight, a shiver runs down my spine. There's something unsettling about it, a weight that seems disproportionate to its size. I pocket it quickly, suddenly eager to be out of these woods and back in the safety of my home.

The trek back feels longer, every shadow seeming to hide potential threats. By the time I emerge from the treeline and see my house in the distance, relief washes over me. All I want now is a hot shower and my bed, to process everything I've witnessed tonight.

But as I approach my front porch, that relief curdles into dread. Something's not right. The front door, which I distinctly remember locking before my stakeout, is now slightly ajar.

I freeze on the porch steps, my mind racing. Did the cloaked figure circle back while I was searching the woods? Or is this someone else entirely? For a moment, I consider calling Charlie or the police. But curiosity and a stubborn determination win out. This is my home, and I'm tired of being scared in it.

Taking a deep breath, I push the door open slowly, wincing at the creak of the hinges. The entryway is dark and still. I fumble for the light switch, my hand shaking slightly. As warm light floods the room, I brace myself for... what? An attacker? More arcane symbols?

But the foyer appears undisturbed. Frowning, I move further into the house, flicking on lights as I go. Everything seems normal until I reach the living room. There, I stop short, my blood running cold.

The large mirror above the fireplace, a family heirloom that's hung there for generations, is covered in writing. Red, dripping letters spell out a chilling message:

"LEAVE NOW. THE POWER IS OURS TO CLAIM. YOUR MEDDLING WILL ONLY BRING PAIN."

As I stare at the mirror, my own pale reflection visible between the scarlet words, the reality of my situation crashes over me. This is no longer just a mystery to be solved. It's a threat, a dangerous game with stakes I'm only beginning to understand.

The rational part of my brain notes that the substance looks more like red paint than blood, but that offers little comfort. Someone was in my home, violated my personal space to leave this warning. And given the timing, it's likely connected to the cloaked figure I chased through the woods.

Chapter 11

I'm still reeling from the night's events, the threatening message on the mirror burning itself into my memory, when there's a sharp knock at the door. My heart leaps into my throat. Has the hooded figure returned? But as I cautiously approach the entryway, I hear familiar voices on the other side.

"Lena? It's Sheriff Mark. Are you alright in there?"

Relief washes over me as I unlock the door, but it's short-lived. Standing on my porch are Sheriff Mark and, to my surprise, Margo Winters. The expression on Margo's face is a mix of concern and excitement that immediately sets me on edge.

"Thank goodness you're okay!" Margo exclaims, pushing past me into the house. "When I saw that... that person skulking around your property, I feared the worst!"

I blink, trying to process this new development. "You saw someone? When?"

Sheriff Mark steps inside, his keen eyes taking in the disarray of my usually tidy living room. "Mrs. Winters called the station about an hour ago, reporting a suspicious figure on your property. Given recent events, I thought it best to check it out personally."

Margo nods vigorously, her perfectly coiffed hair bobbing with the movement. "It was terrifying, Lena. I couldn't sleep, so I was sitting by my window, and that's when I saw it. A hooded figure, moving through your garden like some kind of specter!"

I feel a chill run down my spine. Margo's description matches what I saw during my stakeout. But how much should I reveal? And can I trust Margo's account?

"Did you see where this figure went?" I ask, trying to keep my voice steady.

Margo's eyes widen. "Oh, it was dreadful. They disappeared into the woods at the edge of your property. But not before I got a glimpse under their hood. And Lena, you won't believe who it was!"

I lean forward despite myself, curiosity getting the better of me. "Who?"

Margo lowers her voice dramatically. "It was one of the Blackwood sisters. I'm sure of it!"

The accusation hangs in the air, heavy and unexpected. I exchange a glance with Sheriff Mark, whose expression has grown more serious.

"That's a very serious claim, Mrs. Winters," he says. "Are you certain about what you saw?"

Margo nods emphatically. "Absolutely certain, Sheriff. I'd recognize that wild hair and those beady eyes anywhere. It was definitely one of those so-called 'psychics'. Though if you ask me, the only thing they're good at divining is trouble!"

As Margo continues to elaborate on her sighting, embellishing her story with each retelling, I can't shake a nagging doubt. Something about this doesn't add up. The figure I chased was graceful, almost ethereal in their movements. Nothing like the Blackwood sisters' usual dramatic flair.

But if not them, then who? And why is Margo so eager to point the finger in their direction? As I ponder these questions, I realize that the mystery surrounding my home is far from solved. In fact, it seems to be growing more complex by the minute.

With Margo's accusation still ringing in my ears, I make a split-second decision. If we're laying our cards on the table, it's time to show my hand.

"Sheriff," I say, interrupting Margo's increasingly colorful description of events, "there's something you need to see."

I lead them to the living room, where the mirror still bears its ominous message. The red letters seem to glow in the dim light, a stark reminder of the danger lurking just beyond the walls of my home.

Sheriff Mark's sharp intake of breath is audible in the sudden silence. Even Margo, for once, seems at a loss for words.

"When did this happen?" Mark asks, his voice tight with concern.

I recount the events of my stakeout, the chase through the woods, and my discovery upon returning home. As I speak, I can see the sheriff's expression growing more troubled.

"And you're sure you locked the door before you left?" he presses.

I nod firmly. "Positive. Whoever did this, they either have a key or know how to pick locks."

Mark runs a hand through his hair, a gesture I've come to recognize as a sign of deep worry. "This is serious, Lena. Breaking and entering, vandalism, threats... We need to get to the bottom of this, and fast."

He turns to examine the mirror more closely, pulling out his phone to take pictures of the message. As he does, I notice Margo eyeing me with an expression I can't quite read. Is it concern? Suspicion? Or something else entirely?

"Well," Margo says, her voice unnaturally bright, "I think it's clear what needs to happen next. You need to arrest those Blackwood sisters, Sheriff. They're obviously behind all of this!"

I open my mouth to protest, but Mark beats me to it. "Let's not jump to conclusions, Mrs. Winters. We need evidence before we can make any arrests."

But Margo isn't backing down. "Evidence? What more do you need? I saw one of them sneaking around the property, and now there's this threatening message. It all fits!"

As they argue, I find my gaze drawn back to the mirror. Something about the writing nags at me. The phrasing, the dramatic flair... it doesn't feel like the Blackwood sisters. But if not them, then who?

My thoughts are interrupted by the sound of Mark calling for backup on his radio. "This is Sheriff Reynolds. I need all available units to converge on the Larsen property. We have a potential suspect in the area. Approach with caution."

The gravity of the situation hits me anew. This is really happening. My home, my safe haven, has become the center of a criminal investigation. And as much as I want answers, I can't shake the feeling that we're missing something crucial.

As we wait for the deputies to arrive, I find myself studying Margo. She seems almost... excited by the unfolding drama. It's a stark contrast to my own churning anxiety. What's her stake in all of this? And why is she so convinced of the Blackwood sisters' guilt?

With each passing moment, the tension in the room grows thicker. We're on the cusp of something big, I can feel it. But whether it will bring answers or only more questions remains to be seen.

The sound of approaching sirens breaks the tense silence that has fallen over my living room. Sheriff Mark moves to the window, peering out at the street where red and blue lights now paint the night in alternating hues.

"My deputies are here," he says, turning back to us. "I'm going to brief them on the situation and organize a search for the Blackwood sisters."

As he strides towards the door, Margo hot on his heels with more unsolicited advice, I'm struck by a sudden realization. In all the chaos, I haven't told them about the charm I found in the woods. Should I mention it now? Or keep it to myself until I understand its significance?

Before I can decide, the front door bursts open. Deputy Daniels, a young officer I recognize from around town, rushes in. "Sheriff, we've got a situation outside."

Mark's hand instinctively moves to his gun. "What kind of situation, Daniels?"

The deputy's eyes dart nervously between us. "The Blackwood sisters, sir. They're here. And they've brought Dr. Holloway with them."

For a moment, we all stand frozen, processing this unexpected turn of events. Then, as if a spell has been broken, we're all moving at once. Mark strides purposefully towards the door, Margo hurries to fix her hair in the nearest reflective surface, and I... I just try to steady my racing heart.

As we step onto the porch, the scene that greets us is nothing short of surreal. Bathed in the flashing lights of police cruisers, Evelyn and Eva Blackwood stand side by side, their matching flowing robes billowing dramatically in the night breeze. Beside them, looking distinctly uncomfortable, is Dr. Holloway, still in his white coat as if he'd rushed here straight from his office.

"What is the meaning of this?" Evelyn's voice rings out, dripping with indignation. "Why are we being hunted like common criminals?"

Sheriff Mark steps forward, his stance wary. "Mrs. Blackwood, we have reason to believe you may have been involved in some suspicious activity on Ms. Larsen's property tonight. We'd like to ask you a few questions."

Eva lets out a bark of laughter. "Suspicious activity? Oh, that's rich coming from you lot. If anyone should be answering questions, it's her!" She jabs a bejeweled finger in Margo's direction.

Margo gasps in outrage. "How dare you! I'm not the one sneaking around in the middle of the night, performing who knows what kind of ungodly rituals!"

As the accusations fly back and forth, I catch Dr. Holloway's eye. He looks... nervous. More than the situation calls for. What's his role in all of this?

Sheriff Mark raises his hands, trying to calm the escalating tensions. "Ladies, please. Let's all take a step back and—"

But Evelyn cuts him off. "No, Sheriff. I'm afraid we're well past the point of pleasantries. There's been a grave misunderstanding here, and it's time to set things straight."

Chapter 12

The tension on my front porch is palpable as accusations fly back and forth. I feel like I'm watching a tennis match, my head swiveling from one party to another. But nothing could have prepared me for what happens next.

Evelyn Blackwood, her eyes flashing with righteous anger, points a bejeweled finger directly at Margo. "Enough of this charade!" she declares, her voice ringing out in the night air. "We all know who the real culprit is here. It was you, Margo Winters, who poisoned those innocent people!"

The accusation hangs in the air for a moment, heavy and shocking. I find myself holding my breath, waiting for Margo's response. It comes swiftly and indignantly.

"Me?" Margo scoffs, her voice rising an octave. "That's preposterous! How dare you accuse me when the evidence of your guilt is right there for everyone to see!" She gestures wildly towards my house. "The warning on the mirror! The shadowy figures skulking about! It's obvious to anyone with half a brain that this is all part of your witchy schemes!"

I watch as Margo's face flushes with what looks like genuine outrage. But is it real, or just a masterful performance? My mind races, trying to piece together the conflicting accounts.

Sheriff Mark steps forward, his calm voice a stark contrast to the heated exchange. "Let's all take a breath here. Mrs. Blackwood, that's a serious accusation. Do you have any evidence to support it?"

Evelyn draws herself up to her full height, which is still a good head shorter than the sheriff. "Evidence? Just look at the facts, Sheriff. Who has been obsessed with this property for years? Who would benefit most from Lena being out of the picture? It's not us, I can tell you that much."

As the accusations continue to fly, I can't help but feel like we're still missing a crucial piece of the puzzle. The truth is out there, hovering just beyond our grasp. But which version of events can I trust?

Eva Blackwood steps forward, her expression uncharacteristically serious. "Alright, I suppose it's time for some honesty here." She takes a deep breath, exchanging a glance with her sister before continuing. "Yes, we have been sneaking around the property at night. But it's not what you think!"

I lean forward, intrigued despite myself. "What do you mean?"

Evelyn picks up the thread. "We've been casting protective wards, Lena. Ever since the poisoning at your party, we knew something dark was afoot. We were trying to keep you safe!"

I blink, trying to process this new information. "Protective wards? But why didn't you just tell me?"

The sisters exchange another look, this one tinged with embarrassment. "Well," Eva admits, "we didn't think you'd believe us. Most people don't take our... abilities... seriously."

As much as I want to dismiss their explanation as more new-age nonsense, I can't help but remember the strange energy I felt during my stakeout, the glowing symbols in the air. Could there be some truth to their claims?

Sheriff Mark, ever the voice of reason, interjects. "Let's say for argument's sake that this is true. It still doesn't explain the threatening message on Lena's mirror."

The Blackwood sisters' faces darken in unison. "Oh, we had nothing to do with that," Evelyn says firmly. "But we can guess who did."

All eyes turn to Margo, who takes an involuntary step back. "Now wait just a minute," she sputters. "You can't possibly think-"

"Oh, but we do," Eva cuts in. "It's clever, really. Write a threatening message, point the finger at us 'witchy' types. A perfect way to frame us and fake your own innocence."

As I watch Margo's face, I see something flicker in her eyes. Fear? Guilt? It's gone so quickly I can't be sure.

"Come to think of it," I add, fixing Margo with a hard look. "How did you know about the message on the mirror in the first place? I didn't say anything about it to you."

Margo's indignant sputtering fills the air as she vehemently denies the sisters' accusations. Her face is flushed, her normally perfectly coiffed hair starting to come undone. "This is absurd! Absolutely absurd! I've never heard such ridiculous allegations in all my life!"

Dr. Holloway, who has been uncharacteristically quiet until now, steps forward. He shakes his head, his expression a mix of disbelief and disappointment. "I can't believe what I'm hearing," he says, his voice low. "Margo, I've known you for years. Surely you couldn't have been involved in something like this?"

Something in the doctor's tone must strike a nerve because Margo's eyes suddenly narrow, her posture shifting from defensive to offensive in an instant. "Oh, you'd better believe it, Marcus," she hisses, and I'm taken aback by the venom in her voice. "In fact, you'd better believe all of it, because you were in on it too!"

A collective gasp ripples through our little group. Dr. Holloway's face pales, his mouth opening and closing like a fish out of water. But Margo isn't finished. It's as if a dam has broken, and now there's no stopping the flood of revelations.

"That's right, everyone," Margo continues, her voice rising hysterically. "Your beloved town doctor isn't as innocent as he pretends to be. He was there at the party, remember? Conveniently on hand to 'help' when people started falling ill."

I feel my head spinning as I try to keep up with these new accusations. "Margo, what are you saying?" I manage to ask.

She turns to me, and for a moment, I see a flicker of something like regret in her eyes. But it's quickly replaced by a hard, determined look. "I'm saying, dear Lena, that the good doctor here was my accomplice. He was there to distract people while I handed out the poisoned glasses."

Dr. Holloway makes a strangled sound of protest, but Margo steamrolls right over him. "We were only going to do one glass, you know. That was the plan. But then... well, I got a bit carried away. All those years of slights and petty grievances... it seemed like such a perfect opportunity to settle some scores."

I feel sick to my stomach as the full implications of what Margo is saying sink in. All those people at my party, my friends and neighbors, poisoned because of some twisted scheme and old grudges.

"But our actual goal," Margo continues, seeming almost relieved to be unburdening herself, "was just one specific glass. One particular target."

I nod slowly, the pieces finally starting to come together. "Victor's glass," I say. "That's why he was affected the worst."

But to my surprise, Dr. Holloway shakes his head. He looks defeated, the fight gone out of him. "No," he says quietly. "Victor must have picked up the wrong glass by mistake. That glass... it was meant for you, Lena."

The world seems to tilt on its axis as I process this information. Me? I was the target? But why?

As the full weight of Dr. Holloway's confession sinks in, I feel my knees go weak. Sheriff Mark must notice because he's suddenly at my side, a steadying hand on my elbow.

"You alright there, Lena?" he asks, concern evident in his voice.

I nod mechanically, but my mind is reeling. "I don't understand," I manage to say, my voice sounding distant to my own ears. "Why me? What could you possibly gain by poisoning me?"

The silence that follows my question is deafening. Margo and Dr. Holloway exchange a look that speaks volumes, guilt and resignation written across their faces. It's Sheriff Mark who finally breaks the silence, his voice grim.

"It seems pretty obvious to me," he says, and all eyes turn to him. "With you out of the way, Lena, this house—your inheritance—would finally go up for auction."

The pieces start to fall into place, a picture emerging that's as clear as it is disturbing. I turn to Margo and Dr. Holloway, seeing them in a new, harsh light. "You were planning to buy it," I say, the words tasting bitter in my mouth. "Turn it into that bed and breakfast Margo's always dreamed of."

Dr. Holloway nods, unable to meet my eyes. "It would have solved all our problems," he says quietly. "My debts would be cleared, and Margo would finally have the house she's coveted for so long."

Margo lets out a bitter laugh. "It was the perfect plan. Or it would have been if Victor hadn't mucked it all up by drinking from the wrong glass."

I feel a surge of anger rising within me. "The perfect plan?" I repeat incredulously. "You were willing to kill me for a house?"

"Oh, don't be so dramatic," Margo snaps. "The dose wasn't meant to kill you, just... incapacitate you for a while. Long enough for the bank to foreclose and put the house up for auction."

The casual way she says this, as if plotting my poisoning was nothing more serious than planning a surprise party, makes my blood run cold. I look around at the faces surrounding me—the shocked expressions of the Blackwood sisters, Sheriff Mark's grim determination, the guilty slump of Dr. Holloway's shoulders, and Margo's defiant glare.

"I can't believe this," I say, shaking my head. "All this time, I thought I was going crazy. The weird incidents, the threats, the break-in... it was all you?"

Dr. Holloway at least has the grace to look ashamed. "Not all of it," he admits. "The stuff with the ley lines and the rituals, that was genuinely the Blackwood sisters. We just... took advantage of the chaos to further our own plans."

I turn to the sisters, who look as stunned as I feel. "Is that true?" I ask them. "Were you really just trying to protect the property?"

Evelyn nods solemnly. "We sensed the negative energy surrounding this place. We were trying to counteract it. We had no idea..." she trails off, glaring at Margo and Dr. Holloway.

As the full scope of the deception unfolds before me, I'm struck by a sudden, almost hysterical urge to laugh. It's all so absurd—poisonings and real estate schemes mixed with ley lines and protective rituals. How did my life get so crazy?

But beneath the absurdity, there's a very real sense of betrayal and hurt. These people were my neighbors, people I thought I could trust. And all along, they were plotting against me, willing to risk my life for their own gain.

Sheriff Mark clears his throat, breaking through my swirling thoughts. "Well," he says, reaching for his handcuffs, "I think we've heard enough. Margo Winters, Dr. Marcus Holloway, you're under arrest for attempted murder, conspiracy, breaking and entering, and a whole host of other charges I'm sure the DA will be happy to list for you."

As he begins to read them their rights, I watch Margo and Dr. Holloway being led away. They don't resist, seeming almost relieved that the charade is finally over.

The Blackwood sisters approach me cautiously. "Lena," Evelyn begins, "we're so sorry. We had no idea... if there's anything we can do..."

I hold up a hand, suddenly feeling very, very tired. "Not now," I say. "I just... I need some time to process all of this."

They nod understandingly and retreat, leaving me alone on my porch. Well, not quite alone. Granny's ghost shimmers into view beside me, her expression a mix of concern and relief.

"You okay, kiddo?" she asks softly.

I let out a long, shaky breath. "I don't know, Granny. I really don't know."

As I look out over my property – my home, the source of so much strife and mystery these past weeks – I'm struck by a realization. This isn't the end of the story. It's just the beginning. There are still so many unanswered questions, so many loose ends to tie up.

But for now, in this moment, I allow myself to feel a small sense of victory. The immediate danger has passed. The truth, or at least part of it, has come to light. And I'm still here, still standing.

Epilogue

Two months have passed since the dramatic revelations that turned my world upside down. The dust has settled, quite literally in some cases – I've been busy cleaning every nook and cranny of this old house, as if I could somehow scrub away the lingering memories of betrayal and danger. The criminal proceedings against Margo and Dr. Holloway are ongoing, but that's out of my hands now. Life in New Oslo is slowly returning to normal, or at least as normal as it can be when you live in a house with a ghost and a reputation for attracting trouble.

Today, the air is warm and sweet with the scent of blooming flowers. I'm sitting on the front porch, enjoying the peacefulness that has been so hard to come by lately. The porch swing creaks gently as I sway back and forth, a glass of iced tea sweating in my hand. Charlie sits beside me, her presence as comforting and familiar as the old swing itself.

"You know," Charlie muses, breaking the comfortable silence, "I never thought I'd say this, but I'm actually starting to get used to the idea of Granny being here."

I glance at the empty space on my other side, where I know Granny's ghost is sitting, even if Charlie can't see her. It still amazes me sometimes, the way my best friend has accepted the supernatural elements of my life without batting an eye. Then again, after everything we went through in our first mystery together, a ghost probably seems pretty tame in comparison.

"She says she's getting used to you too," I relay, smiling as Granny makes a face at Charlie.

Charlie grins, raising her glass in a toast to the empty air. "Here's to unlikely friendships, Granny."

Granny chuckles, a sound only I can hear. "Tell her I appreciate the sentiment, but I'd appreciate it more if she'd stop putting her feet up on my coffee table."

I laugh, shaking my head. "Granny says thanks, and also to keep your feet off her furniture."

The banter between my spectral grandmother and my very-much-alive best friend fills me with a warmth that has nothing to do with the summer sun. After everything that's happened, it's moments like these that remind me why I fought so hard to keep this house, this home.

As we sit there, enjoying the lazy afternoon, I can't help but reflect on how much has changed. The Blackwood sisters have been keeping a low profile, but they've made it clear that they're available if I ever want to learn more about the "mystical energies" surrounding the property. I'm not sure I'm ready for that just yet, but I appreciate the olive branch.

The town, too, has been different. There are still whispers and curious glances when I walk down Main Street, but they're tinged with something new – respect, maybe? Admiration? It's as if solving the mystery has given me a new status in New Oslo. I'm no longer just "poor Lena, all alone in that big old house." Now I'm "Lena Larsen, the one who uncovered the truth."

It's a strange feeling, this new notoriety. Part of me misses the anonymity of being just another face in the crowd. But another part – a part that sounds suspiciously like Granny—relishes the challenge. After all, Larsens have never been ones to shy away from a little attention.

"Penny for your thoughts?" Charlie asks, nudging me with her elbow.

I smile, shaking off my reverie. "Just thinking about how different everything is now. How different I am."

Charlie nods sagely. "Nothing like a little attempted murder to put things in perspective, huh?"

We both laugh, the sound carrying across the front yard. It feels good to laugh about it now, even if there's still an edge of darkness to the humor. That's how healing works, I suppose—finding light in the shadows, one chuckle at a time.

Our laughter is interrupted by the sound of a car engine. We look up to see Sheriff Mark's cruiser slowing to a stop in front of the house. My heart does a little flip in my chest, a reaction I'm not quite ready to examine too closely.

"Well, well," Charlie murmurs, a mischievous glint in her eye. "Look who's come calling."

I elbow her sharply, trying to ignore the knowing looks from both her and Granny. "Behave," I hiss, even as I smooth down my hair and straighten my shirt.

Sheriff Mark steps out of the car, tipping his hat in our direction. "Afternoon, ladies," he calls out, his easy smile making my stomach do that flip thing again.

"Hi, Mark," I respond, proud of how steady my voice sounds. "What brings you by? Everything okay?"

He approaches the porch, his expression turning serious. "Actually, Lena, I was hoping I could have a quick word with you. In private, if that's alright."

I feel my body tense involuntarily. The last time Mark wanted to speak to me privately, it was to tell me I was a suspect in a poisoning case. My mind races, trying to think of what could have happened now. Have Margo and Dr. Holloway escaped? Has some new evidence come to light?

"Lena?" Mark prompts gently, and I realize I've been silent for too long.

I nod, perhaps a bit too vigorously. "Of course. Um, let's step inside for a moment."

Once we're in the relative privacy of the living room, I turn to face Mark, bracing myself for whatever news he's brought. "Alright, Sheriff," I say, falling back on formality in my nervousness. "What's going on? I swear, things have been quiet lately. There's no crazy new mystery afoot, is there?"

To my surprise, Mark laughs, the sound rich and warm. "No, no, nothing like that," he assures me, his eyes twinkling with amusement. "Though I have to admit, I'm a little disappointed you'd think that's the only reason I'd come to see you."

I feel my cheeks flush, a mix of embarrassment and... something else. "Oh," I manage, eloquently. "I just thought... with everything that's happened..."

Mark's expression softens. "Lena," he says, taking a step closer. "I didn't come here as the sheriff. I came here as... well, as me. Mark."

My heart is pounding so loudly I'm sure he must be able to hear it. "Okay," I say slowly. "So... Mark. What did you want to talk about?"

He takes a deep breath, and I'm struck by the realization that he seems almost as nervous as I feel. "Well," he begins, "I was hoping that now things have died down a bit, you might consider... that is, if you're interested... maybe we could go out to dinner sometime?"

For a moment, I'm sure I must have misheard. Sheriff Mark—confident, capable, handsome Mark—is asking me out? On a date?

"Lena?" he prompts again, and I realize I've gone silent for the second time in as many minutes.

"Yes," I blurt out, perhaps a bit too enthusiastically. Then, trying to regain some semblance of composure, I add, "I mean, yes. That would be nice. I'd like that."

The smile that breaks across Mark's face is like the sun coming out from behind a cloud. "Great," he says, sounding genuinely pleased. "How about Friday? I know a great little place in the next town over. Might be nice to get away from the New Oslo gossip mill for an evening."

I nod, already imagining the explosion of rumors that will follow if we're seen having dinner together in town. "Friday sounds perfect."

As Mark leaves, promising to pick me up at seven on Friday, I feel like I'm floating. It's not until I hear Charlie's excited squeal from the porch that I remember I have an audience.

I step back onto the porch in a daze, my mind still reeling from what just happened. Charlie is practically bouncing in her seat, her eyes wide with excitement.

"Well?" she demands the moment I'm within earshot. "What did he want? Why do you look like you've seen a ghost? No offense, Granny," she adds to the empty air beside her.

I can't help but laugh at her enthusiasm. "He, uh... he asked me out. On a date. This Friday."

Charlie lets out another squeal, this one even louder than the first. "I knew it! Didn't I tell you? Didn't I say he's been making eyes at you for weeks?"

I feel my cheeks flush again. "You might have mentioned it once or twice," I admit.

Granny's ghost is beaming, her spectral form practically glowing with approval. "It's about time," she says. "That boy's been sweet on you since you moved back. I was beginning to think I'd have to arrange an 'accidental' meeting myself."

I relay Granny's words to Charlie, who bursts into laughter. "Oh man, can you imagine? Granny playing matchmaker from beyond the grave?"

As Charlie and I dissolve into giggles, with Granny looking on in amused exasperation, I'm struck by how normal this all feels. Sitting on my front porch, laughing with my best friend and my ghostly grandmother, excited about an upcoming date – it's a far cry from the chaos and danger of the past few months.

"So," Charlie says once we've calmed down a bit, "what are you going to wear? Where's he taking you? Have you thought about how you're going to do your hair?"

I hold up my hands in mock surrender. "Whoa, slow down there. The date's not until Friday. We've got plenty of time to figure all that out."

But even as I say it, I can feel the excitement bubbling up inside me. It's been so long since I've been on a proper date, let alone one with someone I actually like and respect.

"Don't you worry, dear," Granny chimes in. "Between the three of us, we'll have you looking like a million bucks. That sheriff won't know what hit him."

As Charlie and Granny—using me as their medium—start debating the merits of various outfit choices, I lean back in the porch swing and let their chatter wash over me. For the first time in a long time, I feel truly hopeful about the future.

Yes, there are still mysteries surrounding this house. Yes, the events of the past few months have left their mark. But right now, in this moment, I'm not Lena Larsen, amateur sleuth and reluctant ghost whisperer. I'm just Lena, a woman excited about a date with a good man.

And you know what? That feels pretty darn good.

Also by Sloane Finley

Death by Dessert Series
Death by Chocolate Cupcake[1]
Death by Devil's Food Cake[2]

Ghostly Gumshoe Series
Granny's Ghost and the Haunted Homicide[3]
Granny's Ghost and the Poisoned Punch[4]
Granny's Ghost and the Bake-Off Bribe[5]
Granny's Ghost and the Deadly Dinner Party[6]
Granny's Ghost and the Movie Night Murder[7]
Granny's Ghost and the Murdered Medium[8]
Granny's Ghost and the Basement Burial[9]

---

1. https://www.amazon.com/Death-Chocolate-Cupcake-Dessert-Mystery-ebook/dp/B0DPGS8S8Z
2. https://www.amazon.com/gp/product/B0DR7GTS38
3. https://www.amazon.com/gp/product/B0DFZR8LV6
4. https://www.amazon.com/gp/product/B0DGNN9QNK
5. https://www.amazon.com/gp/product/B0DHB1CBQL
6. https://www.amazon.com/gp/product/B0DJ7PW47X
7. https://www.amazon.com/gp/product/B0DJQ4R3L1
8. https://www.amazon.com/gp/product/B0DKB6Y47K

Granny's Ghost and the Murdered Magician[10]
Granny's Ghost and the Deadly Delphinium[11]
Granny's Ghost and the Killer Caroler[12]
Granny's Ghost and the Fatal Fashion Show[13]
Granny's Ghost and the Cook-Off Killer[14]
Ghostly Gumshoe Collection (Books 1 - 3)[15]

Fur-ensic Files Series
Fetch Me a Felon[16]
Best in Show, Worst in Murder[17]
Dachshund Dynasty[18]
Fur-ensic Files Complete Collection (Books 1 - 3)[19]

---

9. https://www.amazon.com/gp/product/B0DL3GRP97
10. https://www.amazon.com/gp/product/B0DLVJJJ33
11. https://www.amazon.com/gp/product/B0DMYJ5RQ6
12. https://www.amazon.com/gp/product/B0DNY9H8YM
13. https://www.amazon.com/gp/product/B0DQHXXW7Z
14. https://www.amazon.com/gp/product/B0DRWFBDK4
15. https://www.amazon.com/Ghostly-Gumshoe-Collection-Paranormal-Mystery-ebook/dp/B0DHPDBYQ9
16. https://www.amazon.com/gp/product/B0DFVQMWV5
17. https://www.amazon.com/gp/product/B0DHPWBRFT
18. https://www.amazon.com/gp/product/B0DJG9KWYL
19. https://www.amazon.com/Fur-ensic-Files-Collection-Sloane-Finley-ebook/dp/B0DJZV9ZLZ

www.ingramcontent.com/pod-product-compliance
Ingram Content Group UK Ltd.
Pitfield, Milton Keynes, MK11 3LW, UK
UKHW021013180825
7441UKWH00015B/74

9 798231 581771